The True Story of
Peter Rabbit

Eastwood Dunkeld
Sep 4th 93

My dear Noel,
I don't know what to write to you, so I shall tell you a story about four little rabbits whose names were—

Flopsy, Mopsy, Cottontail

and Peter.

They lived with their mother in a sand bank, under the root of a big fir tree.

but Flopsy, Mopsy, and Cottontail had bread and milk and blackberries for supper.

I am coming back to London next Thursday, so I hope I shall see you soon, and the new baby. I remain, dear Noel, yours affectionately Beatrix Potter.

Mr McGregor came up with a basket which he intended to pop on the top of Peter, but Peter wriggled out just in time, leaving his jacket behind.

ran straight away to Mr McGregor's garden and squeezed underneath the gate.

First he ate some lettuce, and some broad beans, then some radishes, and then, feeling rather sick, he went to look for some parsley; but round the end of a cucumber frame whom should he meet but Mr McGregor!

and this time he found the gate, slipped underneath and ran home safely.

Mr McGregor was planting out young cabbages but he jumped up + ran after Peter waving a rake + calling out 'Stop thief'.

and the other shoe amongst the potatoes. After losing them he ran on four legs + went faster, so that I think he would

Peter was most dreadfully frightened + rushed all over the garden for he had forgotten the way back to the gate. He lost one of his shoes among the cabbages

have got away altogether, if he had not unfortunately run into a gooseberry net and got caught fast by the large buttons on his jacket. It was a blue jacket with brass buttons; quite new.

'Now, my dears', said old Mrs Bunny 'you may go into the field or down the lane, but don't go into Mr McGregor's garden'.

Mr McGregor hung up the little jacket + shoes for a scarecrow, to frighten the black birds.

Flopsy, Mopsy + Cottontail, who were good little rabbits went down the lane to gather blackberries, but Peter, who was very naughty

Peter was ill during the evening, in consequence of over eating himself. His mother put him to bed and gave him a dose of camomile tea,

A Note About the Endpapers

The front endpapers are a facsimile of the original picture letter sent by
Beatrix Potter to Noel Moore in 1893. The back endpapers show this same letter but
cleaned for greater legibility and laid out in the correct reading order.

The True Story of Peter Rabbit

How a Letter from Beatrix Potter Became a Children's Classic

by JANE JOHNSON

Originally published as
My Dear Noel: The Story of a Letter from Beatrix Potter

PUFFIN BOOKS

For my mother

PUFFIN BOOKS
Published by the Penguin Group
Penguin Young Readers Group, 345 Hudson Street, New York, New York 10014, U.S.A.
Penguin Group (Canada), 90 Eglinton Avenue East, Suite 700, Toronto, Ontario, Canada M4P 2Y3 (a division of Pearson Penguin Canada Inc.)
Penguin Books Ltd, 80 Strand, London WC2R 0RL, England
Penguin Ireland, 25 St Stephen's Green, Dublin 2, Ireland (a division of Penguin Books Ltd)
Penguin Group (Australia), 250 Camberwell Road, Camberwell, Victoria 3124, Australia (a division of Pearson Australia Group Pty Ltd)
Penguin Books India Pvt Ltd, 11 Community Centre, Panchsheel Park, New Delhi - 110 017, India
Penguin Group (NZ), Cnr Airborne and Rosedale Roads, Albany, Auckland 1310, New Zealand (a division of Pearson New Zealand Ltd)
Penguin Books (South Africa) (Pty) Ltd, 24 Sturdee Avenue, Rosebank, Johannesburg 2196, South Africa

Registered Offices: Penguin Books Ltd, 80 Strand, London WC2R 0RL, England

First published in the United States of America under the title MY DEAR NOEL: The Story of a Letter from Beatrix Potter,
by Dial Books for Young Readers, a division of Penguin Young Readers Group, 1999
Published by Puffin Books, a division of Penguin Young Readers Group, 2006

1 3 5 7 9 10 8 6 4 2

Copyright © Jane Johnson, 1999

THE LIBRARY OF CONGRESS HAS CATALOGED THE DIAL BOOKS FOR YOUNG READERS EDITION AS FOLLOWS:
Johnson, Jane.
My dear Noel : the story of a letter from Beatrix Potter / Jane Johnson.—1st ed.
p. cm.
Summary: A letter from Beatrix Potter to a young friend who is ill marks the origin of her famous tales.
ISBN: 0-8037-2050-5 (hardcover)
1. Potter, Beatrix, 1866–1943—Correspondence—Juvenile literature.
2. Women authors, English—20th century—Correspondence—Juvenile literature.
3. Women artists—Great Britain—Correspondence—Juvenile literature.
4. Moore, Noel—Correspondence—Juvenile literature.
[1. Potter, Beatrix, 1866–1943. 2. Moore, Noel. 3. Letters.] I. Title.
PR6031.072M9 1999 823'.912—dc20 [B] 96-11074 CIP AC

Pages 38–39: The endpapers from *The Tale of Peter Rabbit* by Beatrix Potter
Copyright © Frederick Warne & Co., 1902, 1987
Reproduced by kind permission of Frederick Warne & Co.

The picture letter from Beatrix Potter to Noel Moore, 4 September 1893
Copyright © Frederick Warne & Co., 1946
Reproduced by kind permission of Frederick Warne & Co.

Frederick Warne & Co. is the owner of all rights, copyrights,
and trademarks in the Beatrix Potter character names and illustrations.

The author gratefully acknowledges Judy Taylor's book Letters to Children,
*published by Frederick Warne, 1992, for its invaluable information regarding the Moore family.
The art was rendered in pen-and-ink and watercolor.*

Puffin Books ISBN 0-14-240789-5

Manufactured in United States of America

"Miss Potter's coming today!" shouted Noel as he tumbled out of bed to tell the others.

All the Moore children loved Miss Potter's visits. But Noel had known her longest, so he felt she belonged to him more than to Eric or Marjorie or Freda.

She spent so many hours alone in her room at the top of a big
silent house that Noel was sure Miss Potter had much more fun with
his family.

"Mama, is Miss Potter having *her* breakfast now?" Noel asked.

Before she could answer, the others began: "Will she bring her mice?" "I want to stroke her rabbit!"

"Wait and see; and don't all talk at once, dears."

When Noel had finished lessons with Mama, Nanny fetched the children's hats and they all streamed through the garden gate onto the common.

I must find something to give Miss Potter, Noel thought.

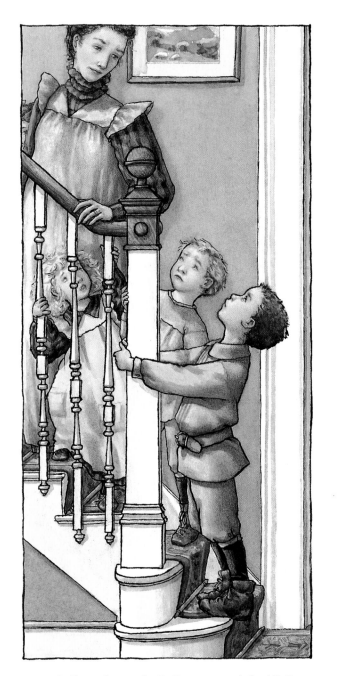 

After lunch Mama said, "Now we'll have a rest before Miss Potter comes," and though they fussed, she bundled everyone up to bed.

As Noel's eyes closed, he murmured, "Miss Potter's on her way."

"Oh, it's *lovely* to see all of you!" cried Miss Potter, running up the path. "Is this for me, Noel? What a wonderful color. I shall wear it in my hat."

Then, opening Miss Potter's packages, they discovered treats for everyone—even the new baby who had not yet arrived.

Miss Potter's rabbit, Peter, and her mice forgot the tricks she'd taught them and were naughty instead.

Miss Potter laughed, the children shrieked, and no one scolded.

She told jokes that made them ache with giggles.

She drew pictures and never said, "I'm tired, that's enough!"

Later, when Noel had Miss Potter to himself, she whispered, "I am going to Scotland soon, so I shan't see you for a while. But I *shall* write."

When the time came, Noel could hardly bear to see Miss Potter go.
After a last good-bye, Mama said, "Now, I expect you all to tidy up."
"I'm hot, and my head hurts," grumbled Noel.

"It might just be the excitement, and too much cake," said his mother anxiously.

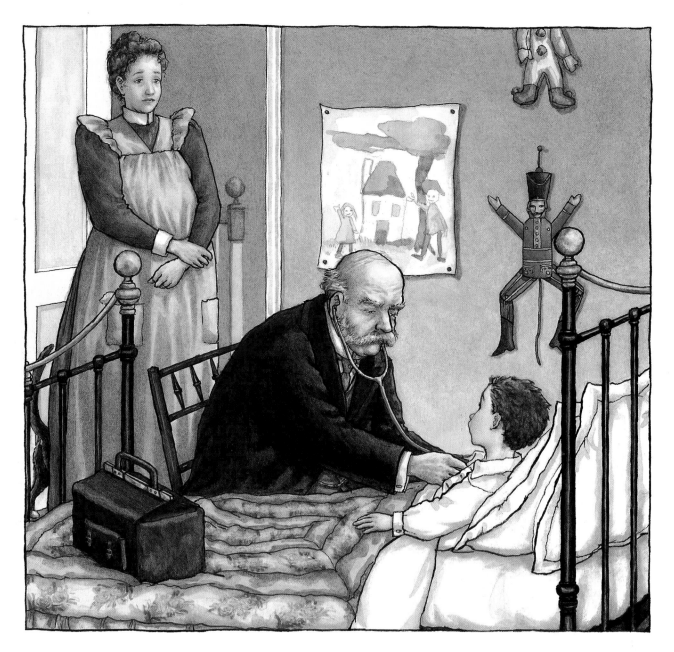

But in the morning Noel was worse, and because he was often ill,
he knew he'd have to stay in bed a long, long time.

Slowly the days dragged by. Gazing out of the window, Noel
listened to the sounds of breakfast, lessons, and then the shouts on
the common as the others played.

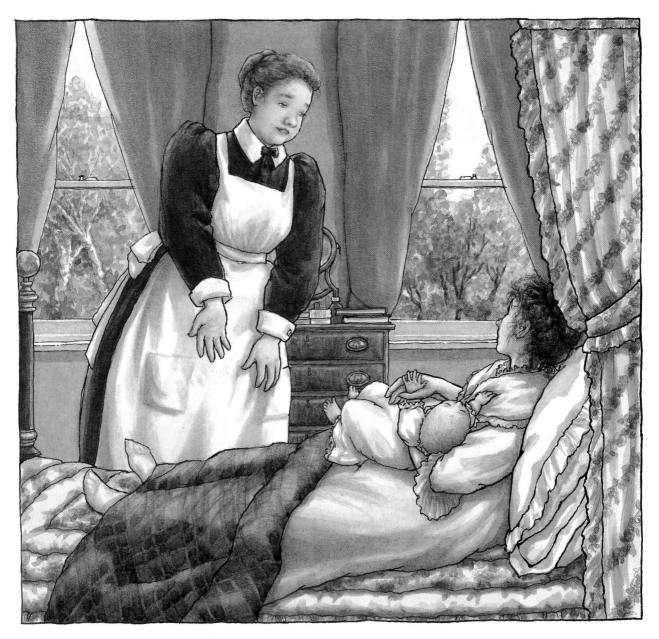

"Miss Potter would know how to cheer him, Mrs. Moore—I'm kept so busy with the younger ones," said Nanny.

"And I'm worn to a rag with Baby," replied Mama.

All summer long Noel lay in bed, forgetting how it felt to be well.
Sometimes he cried when no one heard him call. Sometimes he slept.

At last, with autumn in the air, a letter came for him.
"See, darling, a fat envelope, full of Miss Potter's news."

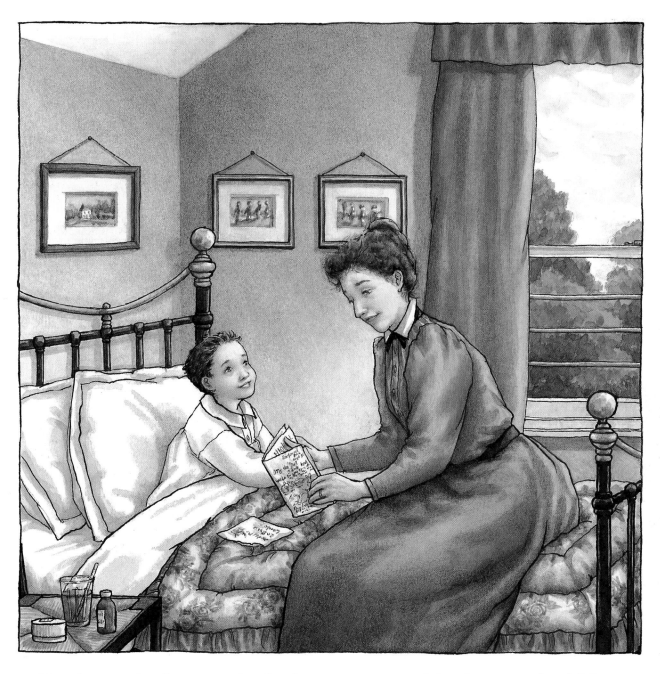

But instead of news, she had sent a *story*, with pictures. And Mama stayed, reading it over and over until she was hoarse.

"It's about a rabbit family, but it's just like ours!" exclaimed Noel as the tale began with a mother rabbit and her children. Then, listening to the adventures of the hero, Peter Rabbit, he decided, "It's really about *me*!"

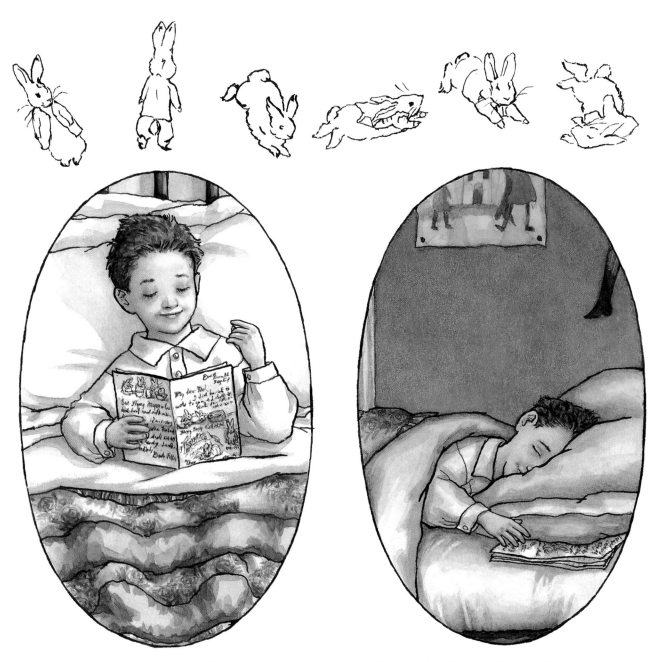

Soon Noel knew the story by heart. He read it to himself whenever he was lonely. It made him laugh. At night he dreamed that he was Peter Rabbit, and woke remembering how it felt to run. He wanted to be well.

Within a week he was getting better, and Miss Potter was back.

"You made that story up specially for me?" Noel's eyes grew dark and round as he gazed at his visitor. "Are we best friends?"

Miss Potter smiled. "Of course we are," she said gently. "Best friends."

Noel Moore was a real little boy who lived in London on the edge of Wandsworth Common, a public park. He was five in 1893 when Miss Potter wrote her first story for him. A few years later he was ill again, with polio, and always afterward walked with a limp.

Quite soon there were eight children in the Moore family, and the house was full. Once she had begun, Miss Potter went on writing stories for Noel, Eric, and the babies as they grew.

At length, Mrs. Moore had an idea that the tales might be made into books, for other children to enjoy. Pleased with this thought, Miss Potter asked if Noel had kept the very first one. And Noel, who had treasured it for seven years, lent her his letter. With the story made longer, and with new, colored illustrations, *The Tale of Peter Rabbit* was published in 1902.

Although Miss Potter's stories made her famous, she never forgot the Moores, who had been her friends when she was lonely and unknown. Noel grew up to become a priest, helping children in the slums of London, and was working among young people at the end of his long life.

Children still read the tales of Beatrix Potter. Perhaps she would never have written them if she had not once known and understood a little boy who needed her. Though far from him, she found the way to reach him, and to reach children all over the world.

Eastwood Dunkeld
Sep 4th 93

My dear Noel,
        I don't know what to
write to you, so I shall tell you a story
        about four little rabbits.
                whose names were —

Flopsy, Mopsy Cottontail
                        and Peter

They lived with their mother in a
sand bank, under the root of a
big fir tree.

"Now, my dears," said old Mrs Bunny
"you may go into the field or down
the lane, but don't go into Mr McGregor's
garden."

Flopsy, Mopsy & Cottontail, who were good
little rabbits went down the lane to gather
blackberries, but Peter, who was very naughty

ran straight away to Mr McGregor's garden
and squeezed underneath the gate.
        First he ate some lettuce,
and some broad beans,
then some radishes, and
then, feeling rather sick,
he went to look for
some parsley; but
round the end of a
cucumber frame
whom should he meet but Mr McGregor!

Mr McGregor was planting out young cabbages
but he jumped up & ran after Peter waving
a rake & calling out "Stop thief!"

Peter was most dreadfully frightened &
rushed all over the garden, for he had
forgotten the way back to the gate.
He lost one of his shoes among the cabbages

and the other shoe amongst the potatoes.
After losing them he ran on four legs &
went faster, so that I think he would

have got away altogether, if he had not
unfortunately run into a gooseberry net
and got caught fast by the large buttons
on his jacket. It was a blue jacket with
brass buttons; quite new.

Mr McGregor came up with a basket which
he intended to pop on the top of Peter,
but Peter wriggled out just in time,
leaving his jacket behind,

and this time he found the gate,
slipped underneath and ran home
safely.

Mr McGregor hung up the little jacket &
shoes for a scarecrow, to frighten the
black birds.

Peter was ill during the evening, in consequence
of over eating himself. His mother put him to
bed and gave him a dose of camomile tea,

but Flopsy, Mopsy, and Cottontail
had bread and milk and blackberries
for supper.   I am coming
back to London next Thursday, so
I hope I shall see you soon, and
the new baby. I remain, dear Noel
yours affectionately Beatrix Potter